Jo Ellen Bogart

The Night the Stars Flew

Ginette Beaulieu

For Evie — Let nature light your way — Jo Ellen Bogart

North Winds Press

A Division of Scholastic Canada Ltd.

The paintings in this book were created in oils on linen canvas.

This book was designed in QuarkXPress, with type set in 18 point ITC Cushing Book.

National Library of Canada Cataloguing in Publication Data

Bogart, Jo Ellen, 1945-
The night the stars flew

ISBN 0-439-98866-7

I. Beaulieu, Ginette, 1954-   . II. Title.

PS8553.0465N53 2001   jC813'.54   C2001-930275-4
PZ7.B64Ni 2001

5 4 3 2 1   Printed and bound in Canada   1 2 3 4 /0

To nature lovers of all ages.
— *Jo Ellen*

To Raphaëlle, and to all children who are curious about this planet.
— *Ginette*

Millie lived in a tall house by a small lake. Her bedroom was on the third floor, way up under the eaves. From her window, she could see the branches near the tops of the trees. She could spy on squirrels as they reached for the best pine cones. She could look right into the faces of tiny black-eyed birds.

Millie's favourite tree was a young maple, grown tall and thin from reaching for the sunlight. She loved the way its slender branches looked at night, against the gentle glow of the lake and sky.

One warm summer night, long after going to bed, Millie slipped to the window to watch the twinkling stars through the branches of her maple tree. In the darkness, she noticed something strange. On a branch, very close to the window, was a tiny spot of light. It was pale and bluish and didn't look like anything Millie had ever seen before.

Millie pressed her nose against the screen and stared hard at the tiny spot. Could it be moonlight shining on a tiny drop of water? No, the moon was just a sliver and it hadn't rained for days. She blinked her eyes hard and looked again. The strange light was still there.

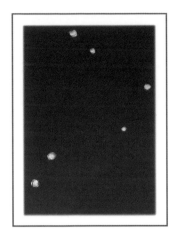

Millie raced down the stairs to tell her parents about the spot of light. "It must be a star shining through the branches," her mother told her. "Now go to sleep."

"Go back to bed, Millie," said her father.

Millie tried to sleep, but couldn't. She kept getting up to see whether the little light was still there. It always was. Finally, she thought of her flashlight. She aimed its beam of light through the screen at the tiny glowing spot. There, on the branch, Millie saw a little striped insect. She turned the flashlight off . . . and the glowing spot was back!

Millie was very curious, but she decided not to bother her parents again. They were never as curious as Millie.

At breakfast, she told her mother, "It was a bug."

"What was a bug?" asked her mother.

"Don't you remember?" asked Millie. "The little light on the branch. It was a bug. I looked at it with my flashlight."

"That's my Millie," said her mother, smiling as she handed Millie some orange juice.

"Do you like bugs?" Millie asked her father. "Can you help me find out about bugs?"

"Well, I'm pretty busy right now, Millie." He sipped his coffee and turned the page of his newspaper.

Millie slumped in her chair and stirred the spoon around in her empty bowl.

When Millie went to bed that night, it was still light. She told stories to her stuffed pig to stay awake. When it was finally dark, she tiptoed to the window to look for the spot of light.

What Millie saw made her mouth fall open. She stared for a moment in wonder, then ran downstairs to tell her parents. This time they'd have to come and see.

"Come look out my window!" she yelled. "The sky is full of little lights. It looks like the stars are flying."

"I'm right in the middle of something, Millie," said her father, tapping at the keyboard of his computer.

"Then come outside," she said, and pulled her father by the hand. "You have to see it, Daddy. You too, Mommy."

The three of them stepped
out onto the front porch.
Floating all through the dark
shapes of the branches were
tiny points of cool white
light. They blinked on and off
as they streaked though the
darkness like meteors.

"See, Mommy?" said
Millie. "It's like flying stars."

"It's so beautiful," said
Millie's father. "They're
fireflies, Millie, and there
must be thousands of them."

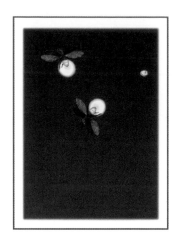

"I haven't seen so many fireflies at once since I was a little girl," said Millie's mother. "My grandma used to call them lightning bugs. On summer evenings my brother and I would run though the meadow by Grandma's house, catching them in our hands."

"I can catch one, too," said Millie. She brought her hands together around one of the moving lights. "I've got one," she said. Millie opened her fingers a crack and peeked at the insect. "Look! His belly is like a bright light! How does he do that?"

"I don't know," said Millie's dad. "I wish I did know."

"His feet tickle!" Millie said, laughing. The firefly crawled across her hand, then lifted its wings and flew away.

"I remember one summer camping with my dad," said Millie's father. "On a hot evening without a breath of a breeze, the fireflies came out, just like now. This night even smells the same."

Millie's mother sighed. "And I remember watching fireflies from my bed on the screened porch at Grandma's."

"Come on, let's see if they're down by the lake," said Millie.

When they got to the shore, Millie pointed and shouted, "They're here! They're here, too!"

The still, dark water reflected a thousand tiny dancing lights.

Millie's mother slipped off her sandals and stepped into the shallow water.

"Me too," said Millie, and waded in.

"Well, I'm not going to be the only dry one," said Millie's father, laughing, and he took off his shoes and socks. "Oh, it's nice and cool," he said, wiggling his toes.

Millie and her mother and her father walked along in the water, holding hands. "I like being out at night," said Millie. "Everything looks different, and special."

"It does look different," said Millie's father, wrapping her in a big hug. "Everything looks very different." He brushed her hair softly from her face.

"Thank you for showing us the fireflies," Millie's mother said.

"Do you still want to learn about bugs, Millie?" her father asked. "We can start by finding out all about fireflies, together."

"Oh, yes," said Millie, nodding.

"Who's for a nice soft bed?" asked Millie's mother.

"Me," said Millie, yawning. Her father gathered her up into his arms and she laid her cheek against his.

With a sleepy, happy smile on her face,
she whispered, "Good night, flying stars."